# THE GREAT BALL GAME

◄ A MUSKOGEE STORY ►

*retold by* JOSEPH BRUCHAC ◄ *illustrated by* SUSAN L. ROTH

*Dial Books for Young Readers*  New York

*Dedicated to the memory of Louis Littlecoon Oliver, Muskogee weaver of stories*
J.B.

*To Janet Vultee, with love and appreciation*
S.L.R.

Special thanks to Kay Kenyon of The Smithsonian Institution Libraries, National
Zoological Park Branch, Washington, D.C.; Dr. Tom Venuum of The Smithsonian;
Kira Muller of the Lacrosse Foundation and the Lacrosse Hall of Fame Museum in
Baltimore, Maryland; Murv Jacob; and the Georgia Department of
Natural Resources, Wildlife Resource Division. —S.L.R.

Published by Dial Books for Young Readers
A Division of Penguin Books USA Inc.
375 Hudson Street
New York, New York 10014

Designed by Ann Finnell
Printed in Hong Kong by South China Printing Company (1988) Limited
First Edition
5 7 9 10 8 6

Library of Congress Cataloging in Publication Data
Bruchac, Joseph, 1942–
The great ball game : a Muskogee story / Joseph Bruchac ;
pictures by Susan L. Roth.—1st ed.
p.   cm.
Summary: Bat, who has both wings and teeth, plays an
important part in a game between the Birds and the Animals to
decide which group is better.
ISBN 0-8037-1539-0.—ISBN 0-8037-1540-4 (lib. bdg.)
1. Creek Indians—Legends.   [1. Creek Indians—Legends.   2. Indians of North America—Legends.
3. Animals—Folklore.]   I. Roth, Susan L., ill.   II. Title.
E99.C9B88   1994   398.2'089973—dc20   [E]   93-6269   CIP   AC

*The illustrations are rendered in collage using paper collected from all over the world: red umbrella paper from
Thailand, a cranberry colored envelope from Tibet, a blue from Japan, a dark green from Italy, and many other
places. Several kinds of paper were handmade, including the mottled white of the rabbit, made
by Sheila Swan Laufer, and the gray of the squirrel, marbled by the artist.*

Ball games of all kinds were played for centuries throughout the Americas, and sometimes a ball game of some type—lacrosse or hockey or a game similar to soccer—would be played to settle an argument instead of going to war. This story, from the Muskogee (also known as the Creek) Indian Nation that lived in the area we now call Georgia, tells how the animal people once settled a disagreement through such a game.

Written versions of the story of the ball game between the birds and animals abound, not only from the southeast, but also from the northeast and the plains region. Basil Johnston published an Ojibway version of the tale, "Why the Birds Fly South in the Winter," in 1981, and a Cherokee version by Lloyd Arneach entitled "The Animals' Ballgame" appeared in print in 1992.

This version of the tale is based on a story told to me by Louis Littlecoon Oliver, an Oklahoma Muskogee elder. I chose to make the game that is played in the story stickball, a lacrosse-like sport that uses two rackets, one held in each hand. Lacrosse and this southern form of the game originated among the Native nations of North America. —J.B.

Long ago the Birds and Animals had a great argument.

"We who have wings are better than you," said the Birds.

"That is not so," the Animals replied. "We who have teeth are better."

The two sides argued back and forth. Their quarrel went on and on, until it seemed they would go to war because of it.

Then Crane, the leader of the Birds, and Bear, the leader of the Animals, had an idea.

"Let us have a ball game," Crane said. "The first side to score a goal will win the argument."

"This idea is good," said Bear. "The side that loses will have to accept the penalty given by the other side."

So they walked and flew to a field, and there they divided up into two teams.

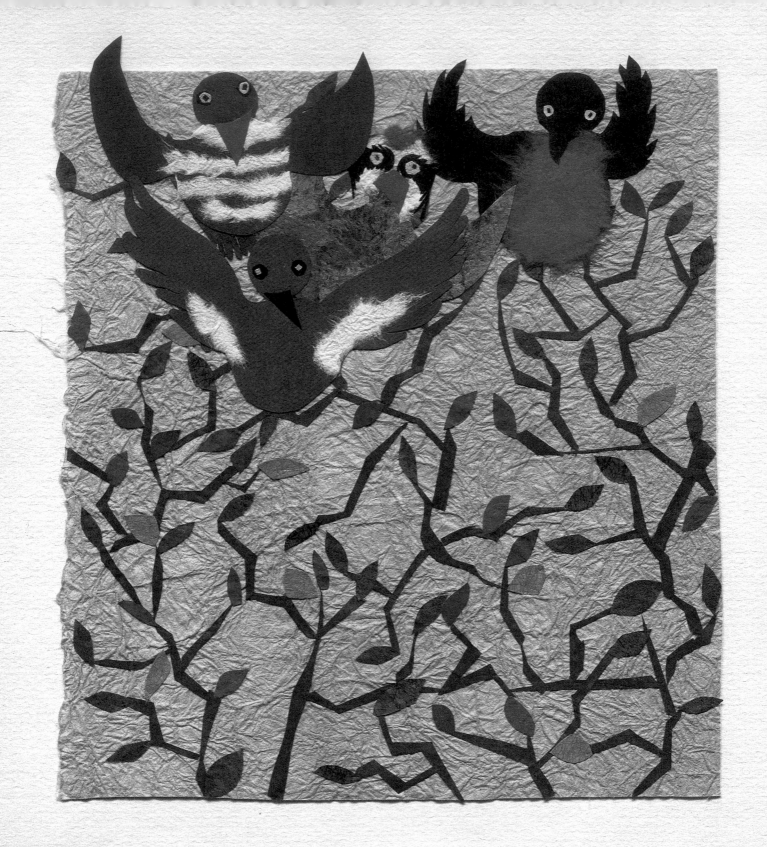

On one side went all those who had wings. They were the Birds.

On the other side went those with teeth. They were the
Animals.

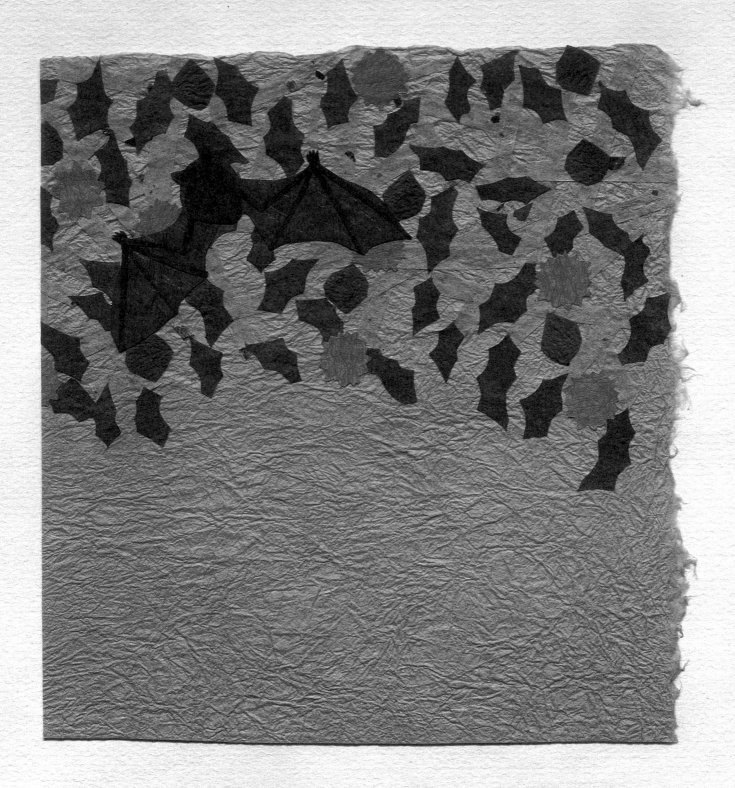

But when the teams were formed, one creature was left out: Bat. He had wings *and* teeth! He flew back and forth between the two sides.

First he went to the Animals. "I have teeth," he said. "I must be on your side."

But Bear shook his head. "It would not be fair," he said.
"You have wings. You must be a Bird."

So Bat flew to the other side. "Take me," he said to the Birds, "for you see I have wings."

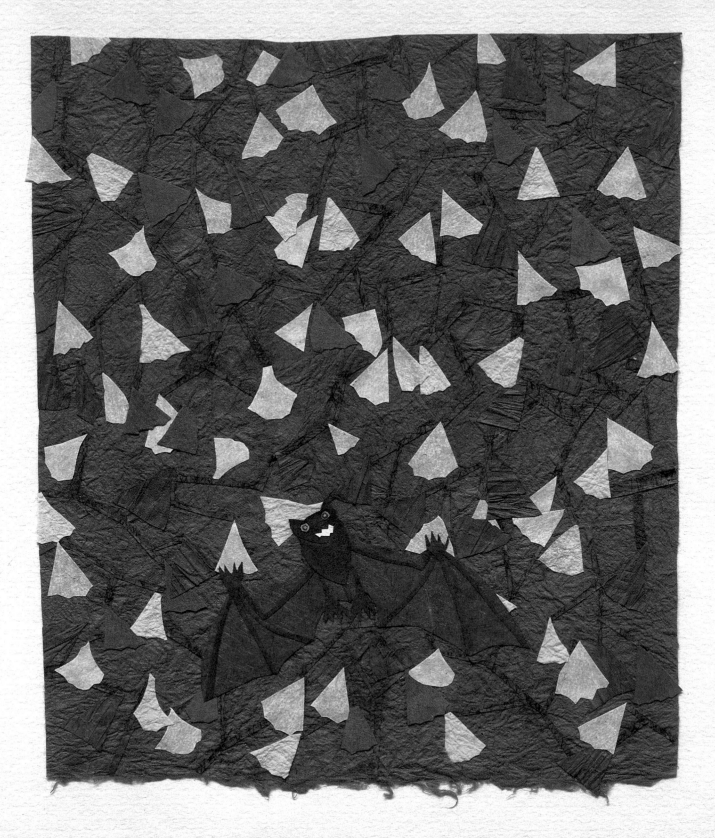

But the Birds laughed at him. "You are too little to help us. We don't want you," they jeered.

Then Bat went back to the Animals. "Please let me join your team," he begged them. "The Birds laughed at me and would not accept me."

So Bear took pity on the little bat. "You are not very big," said Bear, "but sometimes even the small ones can help. We will accept you as an Animal, but you must hold back and let the bigger Animals play first."

Two poles were set up as the goalposts at each end of the field. Then the game began.

Each team played hard. On the Animals' side Fox and Deer were swift runners, and Bear cleared the way for them as they played. Crane and Hawk, though, were even swifter, and they stole the ball each time before the Animals could reach their goal.

Soon it became clear that the Birds had the advantage. Whenever they got the ball, they would fly up into the air and the Animals could not reach them. The Animals guarded their goal well, but they grew tired as the sun began to set.

Just as the sun sank below the horizon, Crane took the ball and flew toward the poles. Bear tried to stop him, but stumbled in the dim light and fell. It seemed as if the Birds would surely win.

Suddenly a small dark shape flew onto the field and stole the ball from Crane just as he was about to reach the poles. It was Bat. He darted from side to side across the field, for he did not need light to find his way. None of the Birds could catch him or block him.

Holding the ball, Bat flew right between the poles at the
other end! The Animals had won!

This is how Bat came to be accepted as an Animal. He was allowed to set the penalty for the Birds.

"You Birds," Bat said, "must leave this land for half of each year."

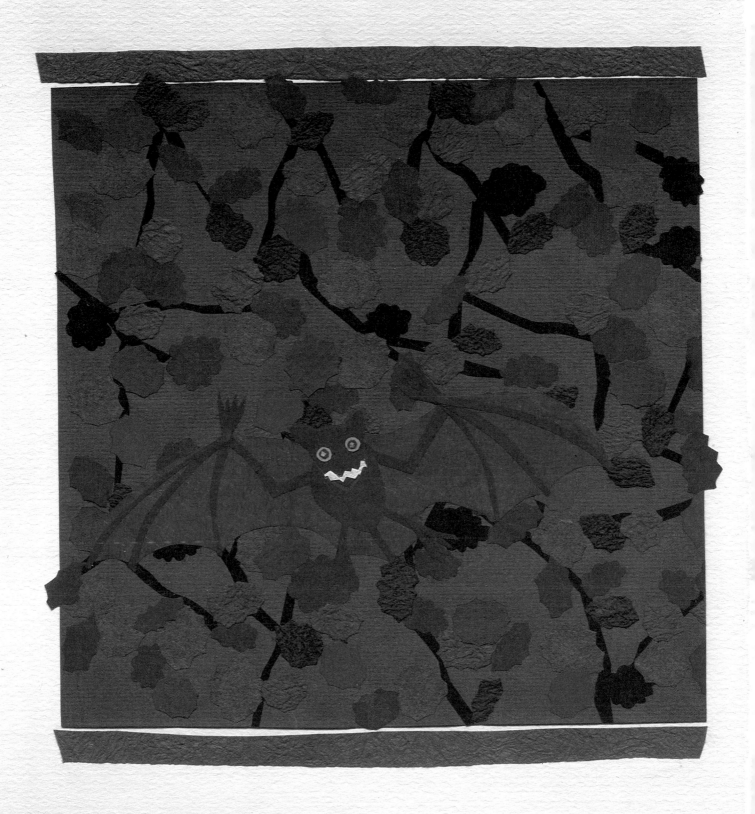

And every day at dusk Bat still comes flying to see if the Animals need him to play ball.

So it is that the Birds fly south each winter. . . .